YEARS OF SOLITUDE

SABHYATA ARORA

Contents

Preface

Unlike other authors, I first thought about the title of the book rather than the story and I eventually came up with 'Years of Solitude'. Using the title, I came up with the story. My thousands of bad ideas led to the good ideas through which I wrote the book. I came up with short scenes and thinking what else I can write about in this book. As the title suggests, it has to do something with solitude. Considering the word 'solitude', I first thought about someone living in solitude and that's what I wrote in the story. I really had to think a lot about what all I can add in the story. I love to give surprises to my readers so the beginning, the ending and the chapters are all full of surprises and twists.

1

The Servant

It was raining heavily, a married couple left their child who had a scar on his forehead near a temple and went away. The next morning, a woman came near that same temple and saw the child crying. She picked up the child and shouted, "Who's child is this?". No one replied. The women then took the child and drove to her house.

In her house, her aunt, Mrs. Jefferson, asked the woman about who's child that was. The woman replied, "I don't know. I found him near the temple. Why don't you and Mr. Jefferson keep him?". Mrs. Jefferson declined to what the woman said. But still, the woman, tried to convince Mrs. Jefferson for the same thing and said, "C'mon, if I didn't have two sons, I would have kept him. You and Mr. Jefferson don't have any kids so you both should take him. Imagine if this child would be yours. He would in New York with you both. The child would get a home to live in."

After a massive conversation between the two of them, Mrs. Jefferson finally agreed to keep the child with her and later told all of this to Mr. Jefferson.

A fortnight later, Mr. Jefferson drove to New York (where he and Mrs. Jefferson lived) along with Mrs. Jefferson and the child. A vast discussion happened on what to name the child after reaching their home. Several names came in both of their minds but they couldn't come up with any name better than 'Gabriel'. "It's pretty nice since I came up with the name."

muttered Mr. Jefferson. When Gabriel was about six and a half years old, his parents (Mr. and Mrs. Jefferson) used to take him to various places in New York. He was lucky enough to visit the whole New York starting from the Statue of Liberty to the National parks and had lots of fun doing so. He enjoyed his parent's company pretty much back then. The boy had an incredible love for his city, New York, and never wanted to live in some other city. He believed and was taught that one should always do what he loves and if he doesn't find anything he likes then find one. "Mistakes are proof that you are trying." is what Mr. and Mrs. Jefferson always told him. While he was growing up, he had zero confidence....and that was his biggest weakness.

At first, Mr. and Mrs. Jefferson were pretty happy that they got themselves a child. But then things started to get worse when Gabriel was treated like a servant by his parents. Little by little, Gabriel's parents forced him to do work when Gabriel was around 15 years old. First, his parents forced him to bring a glass of water. Then they wanted Gabriel to make their bed. Later, they made Gabriel cook food and clean the floor and the windows. He was treated like a complete servant which he really thought it was annoying. His parents used to shout at him so loudly that Gabriel really did not enjoy it.

2
The Locked House

Eight years had passed. After turning 18, Gabriel was continued to be treated as a servant. At this point, Gabriel decided that he would no more live with his parents but live somewhere else. He thought of living alone but he didn't have his own house. Later that day, he heard about a person named 'Belladonna', a scary looking witch who lived near his house. She was popularly known for changing people's lives.

When his mother asked him to bring some vegetables from the nearest grocery store, the clever man, Gabriel, saw his chance and took it. Instead of casually just stepping inside the grocery store, he went to Belladonna's house, hoping that she would change his life and Gabriel could live alone. Since he had no confidence, he was scared to do so but he had no other choice left. He got the money given by his mother for the vegetables which had to be taken and then secretly went to Belladonna's house.

After reaching Belladonna's house, Gabriel rang the doorbell. She opened the door. "Hi," he said "A-Are you Belladonna?".

She nodded. When Gabriel came inside her house, he noticed that the inside walls were painted black. Her house was covered with Halloween pumpkins flying bats and half broken windows.

"Scary" he muttered.

"How can I help you?" asked Belladonna. "Actually" said Gabriel "I've heard you are known for changing people's lives, so I want you to change my life as well."

"And may I ask you why?" she said.

"Well, that's because I don't like my parents anymore. They treat me as a servant. They shout at me and force me to do their work. I want to live alone. Can you make this possible?" he said.

"I'll try." said Belladonna. Belladonna then came near the cauldron she had in her house and started putting various types of chemicals inside it. She then mixed it all with a one-meter-long stick. All she was trying to do was making a potion for Gabriel to drink. She then put some of that potion in an empty bottle and handed it to Gabriel saying, "Now, repeat after me, I'm doing this so that I can stop living with my parents."

Gabriel did exactly what Belladonna told him to do and repeated the same sentence. "Now drink the potion!" she said. He drank the potion and suddenly, slept for 48 hours straight.

When he woke up, everything he saw were doors, walls, paintings and windows. "A house?" he whispered. He came near the main door to open it seemed to be locked.

"Looks like it's a locked house." said Gabriel.

3

The Struggle to Get Out

After Gabriel noticed that the main door was locked, he saw another door that was on the opposite side of the main door. The moment he opened that door, a short-sized robot came out called 'Newt' who followed Gabriel around. "Looks like to open the next door, I need to find a key somewhere here." he said. Later, he found the key right on the edge of the room and headed to the next room. Inside, there was a black cat named Marianne who had a golden coin hanging down her neck with a ribbon. Gabriel came through the door and saw Marianne but then completely ignored her afterwards.

To unlock the next door, Gabriel had to open a safe which was in the same room and it had the key inside it to open the next door. To open the safe, Gabriel had to find a number code. Then he looked around the whole room to find the code but all he found was a piece of paper lying near the safe which had a riddle written on it saying, 'People buy me for eating but never eat me. What am I?' Gabriel was so confused after reading that. He didn't know the answer of that riddle. Then Newt just popped right in front of him with a plate in his hand.

Gabriel saw the plate, held it in his hands and thought that a plate could be the answer of that riddle. But then he questioned himself, "Now what do I do with this plate?". He turned the plate around and saw that code to open the safe. It was 1729. Gabriel then typed that code in the safe and got the key and then he opened the next door. Inside, there was a kitchen table with a microwave kept on top of it.

To find the next key, Gabriel had to insert on next door. He wondered where he could find the golden coin. Then Marianne popped in his mind and he remembered that Marianne had the golden round her neck. So, he ran towards her to get it. The problem was that Marianne was nowhere to be found. Gabriel looked almost all the rooms he had gone till now and there she was, sitting on kitchen table, licking her paw. Gabriel ran towards her to get the coin. When Marianne saw Gabriel running towards her, she got scared and ran through a small hole in the wall where Gabriel couldn't get through. He thought that now there was no way he could catch Marianne and sat down leaning to the wall. At that moment, he started to feel hungry and started to search for some food. He opened the microwave he saw before and a salmon was kept inside. But instead of eating the salmon on his own, he kept the salmon right in front of the small hole Marianne came through so that she would see the salmon, and again come through the hole to eat it. And that's exactly what happened. And then Gabriel quickly took the coin from her and inserted it on the next door.

The moment Gabriel opened that door, the lights of the entire house turned off. When Gabriel took a step forward, something came in his way and he fell on the ground. He then checked what that thing was by which he fell down and it was a torch. He picked up that torch, turned it on and started to look for switch to turn the lights back on but was unable to find it. All he found was a sign on a wall saying, 'Find the key'. Gabriel found neither the light switch nor the key to open the next door. He was starving at this time and also didn't have food to eat.

It took forever for him to find the key but still couldn't find it. He had no other choice left but to kick the door, hoping it would eventually open and so he did.

Now, to get near the next and the last door, Gabriel had to go across the iron nails on the ground and that's what he did. It did hurt him but he had no other choice left with him. After crossing those iron nails, Gabriel got so tired that he literally started crawling on the ground to reach the final door and when he reached it, just like the other doors in the house, this one was locked too. He gave up to find the key to open that door as he was so tired. After that, Gabriel heard a voice. It sounded like someone was opening that door someone was opening it from the outside of that door. When that person opened it, he saw Gabriel lying on the floor and yelled, "Who are you? This is my house. Get out of here!" Newt and Marianne then came towards that person as they had not seen him in a while.

Gabriel then realized that Marianne was that person's pet and Newt was his robot. Later, that person kicked Gabriel out of the house by not knowing who he was. Now that Gabriel was out of the house, he was so happy as he did not enjoy staying in that strange looking house.

4
Years of Solitude

Gabriel now witnessed the fresh air after getting out of that locked house. He noticed that not even a single person was around. He then sat down on a bench nearby and continued to enjoy the fresh air. Meanwhile, two kidnappers, Sam and Bill, both came near Gabriel and stared at him secretly and then decided to kidnap him.

The two of them then spoke to Gabriel for a ransom of a hundered million dollars or else they would kidnap him. Gabriel had some money left with him that his mother gave him for the vegetables he had to buy but he pretended that he didn't have any money left with him because he didn't want to give it to the kidnappers and lied, "I don't have any money." But it did not solve the problem. Actually, the lie worsened the situation when Bill caught his lie and said, "You must have some money, you are lying."

Gabriel couldn't hide his lie anymore and he had to take the money out of his pockets. "This is only $15 and we want $100,000,000." said Sam. Because they didn't get their hundered dollars, they kidnapped Gabriel and took him to a forest. It started to get dark over there. Sam and Bill had a tent with them so they started making it to sleep inside it while Gabriel was making a campfire to cook food. After making the campfire, all three of them started fishing so that they could cook with those fishes with the help of the campfire in order to eat food. Gabriel was terrified spending his time with those two strangers as he had never been with any stranger before.

After eating fishes, the three of them came inside the tent and lied down there. They had no other place to sleep so they tried to sleep there in the tent. Gabriel was facing problem in sleeping as this was the first time he slept in a tent. Sam and Bill were sleeping in a very different manner and snoring so loudly that every animal in the forest must have heard them. This gave an idea that they fell asleep so Gabriel took his chance and escaped from the tent as he didn't want to stay with them.

Gabriel then tried to get out of the forest he was in but he couldn't find his way out.

While he was looking for his way out, he saw the footprints of an animal going straight ahead. Gabriel was not sure which animal's footprints those were and was curious to know so he followed those footprints for a while and it led to a leopard eating a dead tiger. Gabriel was behind it so it didn't see him but the moment he saw the leopard, he was horrified and slowly started moving backwards, not knowing that another animal was waiting for him behind his back. It was an anaconda that was creeping. Gabriel accidently stepped on its face and when he noticed the same, he ran as fast as he could. He eventually, looked behind him to see if the anaconda was chasing him, however, it wasn't. Gabriel anyway hid behind a tree and deeply started to breathe as he was exhausted of running.

The sun started rising. Gabriel again started to feel hungry, even after eating those fishes last night. He started walking around to see if there was any pond nearby so he could catch some more fishes but there was no pond to be found. What he found was buildings, roads, vehicles, houses and even people. It was a city! But he didn't know exactly which city it was but then he somehow found a way to get out of the forest and then reached out to that city. When Gabriel first entered the city, not even a single person was looking at him. He had neither a shelter nor money so he couldn't even buy anything. Yet, the witch, Belladonna, changed Gabriel's life a lot from that potion she gave him. He expected that Belladonna would change his life into something good but instead, she changed his life into a tragedy.

Now that Gabriel had no home to live in, day by day, he started moving around the city to enjoy the places that were free to visit. Voices that's shouting, "Nothing can be done!". He used to visit those places in complete solitude and spent years like that. For the first few months, he thought that now, nothing could be done.

5

The Homeless Man

Now the homeless man, Gabriel, had nothing left to do due to the fact that he was homeless and had no friends and family. He used to see people roaming around with their friends and family while sitting on a footpath. He now regrets drinking the potion which Belladonna offered Gabriel as his life is now a calamity. He used to walk miles for food.

One day, a little boy saw Gabriel sitting on the footpath and thought that he was poor and homeless. He came towards Gabriel, sat beside him and began talking, "Hi, I'm Jordan. What's your name and why are you sitting here?"

"I'm Gabriel Jefferson." Gabriel answered and then told the kid everything that happened to him.

He told him how his parents used treat and then he went to Belladonna and all that. The knew boy knew Belladonna and told this to Gabriel. He said, "Are you talking about Belladonna? I know her. Even I had gone to her house so that she could change my life. I wanted her to change my life from an unintelligent person to an intelligent and hardworking person and she did it."

"Really?!" asked Gabriel "Where is she now?"

Jordan told Gabriel that Belladonna had now shifted from New York to Hammonton, New Jersey and also said that Hammonton was the place where they were currently in. According to Jordan, Belladonna was living somewhere near the Wharton State Forest which was not that far away from where they were currently sitting. Gabriel was pretty upset after knowing that he wasn't in New York anymore.

At that moment, he decided to go to the place where Belladonna was living near that forest and ask her if she could change his life again, even if she had already ruined his life. He decided he would take this risk to see she could make his life any better.

Weeks later, Gabriel finally found his way to Belladonna's home. He reached till the outside of her house and saw a gate. Outside the gate were a couple of watchmen standing with their arms locked. Gabriel asked those watchmen if he could go in to meet Belladonna but one of the watchmen straight-away declined and said that she's busy. Belladonna then came out in her balcony and saw Gabriel right outside her gate. She couldn't recognize him at first but she knew she had seen him before so she quickly phone called one of her watchmen and told them to let the guy in. "Go to the ninth floor, Belladonna's calling you." said the watchman.

By the time, Gabriel reached the ninth floor, he was exhausted as he reached that high up. On the ninth floor, there were ten different rooms and he did not know in which room he had to go in so, he checked every single room up there and when he checked the tenth and final room, he saw Belladonna sitting on her bed and sewing one of her night gowns.

Gabriel cried as hard as he could and said, "W-Where were you? Do you how much I suffered since the last few years. I'm homeless now all because of your potion. Why did you do so?"

Belladonna was shocked to hear that. "Really" she said "Is that actually what happened to you?"

"Of course," he replied "did you really want to change my life into something worse rather than something better?"

Belladonna then remembered the day she first met Gabriel and said, "Oh, I remember you. We first met years ago. You didn't tell me your name."

"I'm Gabriel Jefferson." he said "I trust you. Now, only you can make my life better even if you had already made it worse. I know you are the kind of women who has helped a little kid named 'Jordan'. So, I know you won't do anything bad to me. Please change my life once again. I don't want to be homeless anymore. I want family and friends."

Belladonna clapped. "So, your name's Gabriel Jefferson." she said. "What a nice name. I'm sorry for ruining your life. Even I didn't know that the potion will make your life even worse. I can give you another potion but there is not a hundered percent chance that it will make your life better than ever."

Gabriel was still crying. "I'm ready to drink that potion." said Gabriel "There's still a chance that it would make my life better."

"Okay then." said Belladonna while holding a crystal sphere "I will give you that potion if this crystal sphere says that your future is terrible. But if it says that your future is good then there's no need of this potion. Got it?"

Gabriel happily said "Yes." and stopped crying. Belladonna and Gabriel sat on a chair. Belladonna then kept the crystal sphere on a table which was right in front of her and said, "Hey crystal sphere. I haven't talked to you in a while. I want to talk about Gabriel's future. How will it be?"

Silence.

Belladonna smiled. "What happened?" asked Gabriel. She answered, "It's saying that your future will be full of joy and so many good things will happen that you never expected."

"But it didn't even say anything." said Gabriel.

"It does not say anything." said Belladonna "It whispers and only I can hear it."

"Gabriel didn't believe her and said, "I don't believe you. What kind of whispers are those which only you can hear? "

"Why will I lie?" said Belladonna "Anyways, you don't need the potion."

Gabriel stood up with his hand on the table and said, "I'm leaving and I'll never come back to this place again." He went outside of the room, slamming the door right on Belladonna's face.

Whenever he turned back, he always saw his hometown (New York), and his parents. "I guess I can't go back to the past so I should focus on the present." he said. But circumstances had forced him to think about the past repeatedly. He had decided that he would not go to his hometown back until he makes a big change in his life.

6

The Unexpected Thing

Months passed, while continuing to live in solitude, Gabriel was wondering how he even trusted a woman like Belladonna. He never even believed in witches and all those creatures. So, the question arises, 'How come he trusted Belladonna?'. Well, probably because he was really excited for his life to be changed and didn't really know what else he could do.

While thinking of Belladonna, he bumped his head into a wall and later saw a poster on the same wall. It was about a company. Inside the poster was written about a great proposal of getting a job in that company. He had to do something since he was taught that one should always do what he likes and if he doesn't find anything he likes then find one. "Why can't I be one of those people who are working?" he asked himself "Why can't anything be done?" He didn't have any confidence and so, he brought some. He didn't really have an interest in anything so he decided to find one. And what he was looking for was right in front of him. He could work in the company.

He knew accounting and wanted to make it his new interest. He was anyway homeless so he decided to work there so he could earn enough money that he could buy a himself a house.

In his job interview, the interviewer asked Gabriel a few questions. The first one was, "How did you get to know about this company?"

Gabriel replied, "I was roaming around in a street and I bumped my head right on a wall and later noticed a poster sticking on it which was about this company. I then decided to join this company.

"Why did you want to work here?" asked the interviewer.

Gabriel lied, "Actually, the name of the company is pretty nice and I saw the picture of the company in the poster, it looked pretty good and different so, I decided to join this company."

The truth was that he wanted to just wanted to get a random job and he found this job so he decided to give it a try and work there. "Why should I hire you?" asked the interviewer.

"Well," said Gabriel "People say I'm a hardworking and an intelligent person so I should join a company and work there. Working is my passion and it will always be!". This was again a lie as no one ever said all this to Gabriel. He was just trying to impress the interviewer, hoping that he would hire him. However, the interviewer was not impressed at all. He thought that Gabriel was just a normal person trying to get a job which was true. "I'll tell you later if you are hired or not." said the interviewer "For now, you can leave."

Gabriel got up, walked towards the exit door while crossing his fingers, hoping he would get hired. Instead of walking towards the door, he accidently headed towards a wall and again, bumped his head and fell down. "Ouch!" yelled Gabriel. Meanwhile, the interviewer was confused weather or not to hire Gabriel. He asked his boss about it and…. his boss agreed to hire Gabriel but only if he would work properly and if not then he will be kicked out. The interviewer also agreed, rolling his eyeballs, as like always, he never liked the decision made by his boss but, it was an order so he had to agree. And so, he called Gabriel and said, "Tomorrow morning at the eighth hour, arrive at the office. You are hired." Ending the call straight-away, he didn't even give a chance for Gabriel to speak. "Wait, what did I just hear?" Gabriel asked himself "Am I hired? Unbelievable!" Gabriel was so excited to work there that he forgot the timing he had to arrive at even if, the interviewer had clearly mentioned it in the phone call. So, instead of arriving at 8 in the morning, he arrived at around 10:15 and got scolded by his boss for arriving late on the first day itself. Gabriel, however, didn't mind it, and started doing the work he got.

Before that, he took a step or two inside his beautiful cabin. Then he took a seat and started doing his work. All of this was like a dream for him as he had never been in a big of a company before. On his first day of work, Gabriel met several new people there in the office. Most of them were managers while Gabriel was an accountant. It was his first day so, he was not doing his work correctly. Several mistakes were made by him and he thought that making so many mistakes was normal. His boss unfortunately, didn't have the same thought as Gabriel. He used to hate making mistakes and seeing others do the same. He himself rarely made mistakes. Whenever he got to know that Gabriel made a mistake, he used to yell at him.

After working there in the office for over a month, Gabriel made a massive mistake. And once again, his boss got furious and shouted, "What has happened to you? Why are you making so many mistakes? Don't you know you are working in an office and you can't make mistakes here? If I see you make one more mistake, you can't work here anymore. You'll be fired!"

"Why fired?!" asked Gabriel "Everyone makes mistakes. You can't fire me like that."

"This is my company." replied his boss "And you are just an accountant. So, I can do anything. It'll be my choice, not yours."

"Okay." Gabriel said while making himself louder "But what I was taught when I was a kid is that mistakes are proof that you are trying."

Gabriel left the corridor he stood in and headed towards his cabin, grabbed all his stuff, and stood right outside his office remembering all the mistakes he had done since his first day of work. "Unbelievable! I cannot believe what just happened there." he said to himself "There has to be a solution to avoid mistakes but I don't what it is. I can't just let it be." His inner monologue started to take the name of one of his co-workers, Noah, who was also an accountant and rarely makes mistakes just like Gabriel's boss.

Gabriel's eyes got bigger, he smiled, took out his cell phone from his pocket and phone called.... Noah. In the phone call, he asked how he avoided mistakes. Noah told him that he just did his work carefully and re-checks it before submitting. So that even if he did make a mistake, he could correct it. Right after listening to that, Gabriel immediately ended the call, slowly putting his cell phone down without even looking at it. Something was cooking in his mind. He smirked and left the place.

The next morning, Gabriel came inside his office, straight away headed towards his boss's office and handed his boss some of his work. "Here, I got some of my work done." said Gabriel "Check it." His boss checked it and later asked, "How much time did it take you to complete this work?"

"Five hours." replied Gabriel.

"But this work should've taken you five days to complete considering it was very time taking. How did you complete it in just five hours without any mistakes?" questioned his boss.

"Hard work." said Gabriel to his boss "When I gave an interview for this job, I told the interviewer that people call me hardworking. So, by completing this work in five hours rather than five days, I proved that I'm actually hardworking."

There was just complete silence over there for a second or two. His boss then asked, "Did you do this all by yourself or you took someone's help?"

"No, I would never take someone's help." answered Gabriel "It's my work and of course I will do it by myself."

"Come with me!" said his boss and took him to the corridor which had the greatest number of people. "Everyone, this is Gabriel Jefferson." said his boss to the people standing at large "He works here as an accountant. He used to make a lot of mistakes since the day he first came to this office. But today, he surprised me by completing in five hours. Instead, this work could've taken him five days to complete. I want to appreciate him for his hard work. Can I expect the same from all of you? Can we all stop making mistakes and only focus on the work given to us rather than focusing on some other work during the office hours?"

Everyone standing in that corridor clapped for Gabriel, except Noah, who was also there, looking angrily at Gabriel. Gabriel felt proud and smiled. He then saw Noah and his smile suddenly disappeared. He wondered why Noah was looking angrily at him. Noah left the corridor he was standing in and no one knew where he went. A few hours later, Gabriel was sitting in his cabin doing his work on the computer. He then took a printout of that work as his boss told him to do so.

There comes Noah inside Gabriel's cabin, slamming the door behind him and said, "You cheated by asking me what I do for avoiding mistakes. You asked that so you could copy me. I really didn't expect this from you."

"If you think I cheated then why did you tell all of this to me?" said Gabriel "I had just asked you one thing and if you have a problem in that then I won't ask anything to you ever again. Is that okay?"

"You don't have to ask me anything because I'm anyway not going to answer." said Noah, spilling a glass of water on all the printouts Gabriel took out. "Now what will you do?" asked Noah while smiling. He then left the cabin, leaving Gabriel speechless. Later, Gabriel decided to show up on his boss's cabin in order to tell him that Noah ruined his work by spilling a glass of water on Gabriel's printouts. He did so but, his boss wasn't shocked after hearing that. "Gabriel, is that what you came for?" said his boss "In a business, these kinds of things keep on happening. Don't come to me for these little problems. But it also doesn't mean that you will take revenge by ruining his work. Just do your work better than he does."

"You're right." said Gabriel "I feel foolish as it wasn't even that big of a matter and I was complaining."

He felt more motivated than before to do his work. He then realized that Noah spilled water on his printouts and not his computer. So, he could take those printouts again and show them to his boss. Noah saw Gabriel showing his work to his boss, wondering how it happened even if he spilled water on that same work. Gabriel's boss once again seemed pretty happy as Gabriel completed his work on time without any flaws however, Noah wasn't.

So far, whatever Belladonna told Gabriel was true as she had told him that his future would be full of joy and unexpected things would keep on happening in his life and Gabriel did get pretty happy when he found a job. Getting a new job was also an unexpected thing for him.

7
Lottery Ticket

It was another beautiful day and there was Gabriel, walking towards his office. Suddenly, he looked at something and it made him stop. He saw an old man and woman right outside his office, talking to each other but, this wasn't it. When Gabriel looked at them, something seemed familiar. He looked at them closely but then his eyes rolled out and his jaw dropped and he slowly started stepping backwards. What he saw were his parents, Mr. and Mrs. Jefferson, who adopted him but, Gabriel was never told that he was adopted and thought that they were his real parents.

Gabriel was frightened to see them as he had thought that if they saw him then they would take him back to New York and treat him like a servant. So, Gabriel tried to hide behind a tree so they won't see him. Although, Mrs. Jefferson anyway saw Gabriel, came towards him along with Mr. Jefferson. Gabriel saw them coming towards him and closed his eyes, praying for them to not catch him and started moving away. "Excuse me!" said Mrs. Jefferson to Gabriel "Do you know where the nearest railway station is?"

Gabriel stopped right there. His eyes went wide and was hesitating. It seemed like Mr. and Mrs. Jefferson didn't recognize him, probably because Gabriel kind of looked different. "I-I don't know." said Gabriel.

"You look like our adopted son." said Mr. Jefferson. Gabriel was shocked and said, "Your son's adopted?"

"Yes" answered Mrs. Jefferson while tears were rolling out of her eyes "We don't know what had happened to him. One day, when he was 18, he ran away and never returned."

Gabriel hardened his fists as he was pretty angry after hearing the fact that he was adopted. He was afraid to tell the two of them that their son was standing right in front of him.

Gabriel stepped inside his cabin with a bad mood. He took a chair and sat down with tears in his eyes. The entire conversation that he had with his parents echoed in his own mind which he couldn't get rid of for a long time. Then he thought that it's no time to overthink and so, he got back to work later on.

Within six months of working in the office, the day came when his boss urgently called him in his cabin. He had no idea why his boss called him urgently and was curious to know. He rushed in his boss's cabin and took a seat.

"Hi" said his boss "Good to see you, Gabriel. I need to tell you something you would like to hear. So, the day on which you joined this company to this day, I have seen a change in you. Firstly, you do all your work on time and secondly, you have this passion of working, which I really appreciate. So, I've decided to increase your salary up to 30%. How's that?"

"30%? Nah, you're joking right?" said Gabriel as he couldn't believe that his salary would get increased.

"I'm not." said his boss "Why will I lie?"

"Unbelievable!" muttered Gabriel.

After another three to four months, Gabriel earned a lot of money ever since, his salary got increased. He earned enough money that he could buy a house for himself, and so he did. He bought a house so; he was not homeless anymore. His boss really liked Gabriel's performance and experience of accounting.

Hours passed, then days, weeks, months, and even years. Gabriel achieved excellence in his work. The fact that he was adopted, still kept him disturbed which caused him to make mistakes while working which made his boss furious. His boss had told Gabriel a long time ago that if he made one more mistake then he would be fired. And you won't believe but, that's exactly what his boss did. He suspended Gabriel from his job in front of his co-workers. Everyone was astonished to hear this. Gabriel got the biggest shock. He tried to convince his boss to not fire him but, his boss was not ready to listen a word out of Gabriel's mouth.

Each of Gabriel's co-workers were bothered to know that Gabriel got fired except Noah, who seemed to be happy as he hated Gabriel.

Gabriel met his co-workers for one last time, and said "Goodbye!" to all of them. He took all of his stuff, went out of the office and stared at it for a long time. He was then on his way to home. He kept on walking, keeping the words, 'I am fired. I can't do anything. I'm not worth it.' in his mind until he sees a salesman selling some kinds of tickets. "What kind of tickets are these?" he questioned the salesman.

"Lottery tickets." said the salesman "They cost five dollars each. Wanna buy them?"

Pause.

"And how will I know if I won the lottery?" asked Gabriel.

"Well, to know that, you'll have to go to the mall named 'Jersey Valley' tomorrow at 18:00. They will announce a number that will be written in one of these tickets." he continued "The person who has the ticket containing that number will win a lottery of $50 million."

After hearing that, Gabriel decided to buy one of those tickets. He bought it and held it in his hands and stared at it. His number written on the ticket was 142056. He then quickly kept the ticket inside his pocket and arrived home. "What would happen if I won the lottery?" he kept on wondering regardless of time "Become a millionaire?!"

He kept on wondering till 2 a.m. and eventually fell asleep. It was the next morning and Gabriel couldn't find his ticket. He checked everywhere in his house but, failed to find it. He sat down for a minute and started wondering where it could be but, that did not help at all as his mind turned out to be completely blank and resulted in not remembering anything. He went outside to find the salesman from whom he bought the ticket but, he seemed nowhere to be found.

His eyes opened in the middle of the night, and noticed that it was just a nightmare. His breathing rate became faster and faster as he was terrified after dreaming all of that. "Where did I actually keep my lottery ticket? Oh ya! In my pocket" he pondered while putting his hands in one of his pockets but, the ticket wasn't there. He put his other hand in his second pocket but the ticket wasn't there either. He then remembered that when he got the ticket from the salesman, he was wearing a black trouser and now, he was wearing white. The black trouser was where he kept his ticket. Gabriel then jumped out of his bed, where he was sleeping and searched for that black trouser in his wardrobe, and it wasn't there. He checked his washing machine to see if he accidently kept his trouser there, and he found it. Thankfully, the machine wasn't turned on otherwise, the ticket would also have been washed. He took the ticket out of his pocket, stared at it and once again, smiled. The next evening, Gabriel grabbed his lottery ticket and headed towards the mall 'Jersey Valley'. When he reached inside, a watchman came to him and asking if he was there for the lottery. Gabriel answered, "Yes!" and the watchman took him to a large hall on the second floor and told him that here, the lottery winner would be announced. The hall was super crowded. A cameraman with camera in his hand asked everyone in the crowd about who they think would win the lottery. The most common answers were, "It's hard to tell." and "Probably, the luckiest person."

The cameraman asked the same question to Gabriel at the very last but, Gabriel replied, "It will be me!" Everyone in the hall laughed at him after hearing his answer. A person then came on the stage and said, "Hello everyone! I know that all of you are waiting for the winner to be announced so, I will say a number and the person who has the same number written on their ticket, will win the lottery of $50 million." he continued "So, listen carefully. I'm announcing that number. And the number is..."

There was no speaking in the hall as everybody was excited to know who wins the lottery. The person on stage the announced that number. "142056" he said.

Gabriel screamed, "I won! I won the lottery!"
The person on stage heard Gabriel's shout and said, "Congratulations! I'd like to call you on stage. Please come." Everyone applauded Gabriel on winning the lottery! Gabriel then got on stage and happily showed his ticket to the person who was already there on stage. The person checked the number on Gabriel's ticket and then gave him his winning amount of $50 million. The photographers clicked the pictures of Gabriel when he was taking the winning amount. Those pictures of Gabriel came in newspapers and

Gabriel took a cut out of those pictures, framed and hanged it on his bedroom's wall. It was truly a memorable day for Gabriel.

27

8

Global Enterprises

The alarm clock started to ring. Gabriel turned it off to check the time. It was six in the morning. "Why did I even set the alarm clock since, I don't have to wake up early for work?" he wondered while getting out of the bed. He opened up his curtains and the sunlight brightened his bedroom. He saw people jogging through the window so, Gabriel decided to join them.

Every single person out there was either with one of their family members or their friends however, Gabriel was still living in solitude. He saw two people talking to each other about business. Gabriel came a bit closer to them without them knowing it to hear their talk. What they said was that having a business or any kind of job or something is very important otherwise, life becomes too easy and boring and hard work is important. Their talk influenced Gabriel to find another job for himself. So, Gabriel went on finding a job but failed to find one. Every adult from 22-60 years of age in his neighborhood was working but Gabriel wasn't. Considering the fact that he lived in solitude, he didn't really have anything left to do. Ever since he lost his job, everyone and everything he looked at somehow seemed so indifferent. At this point, whatever he could do in a day was exercising, walking, lying on bed and sleeping because he didn't have much to do and there was no one he could talk to. After another month and a half, Gabriel decided that he couldn't live like this anymore and really had to find some work to do. He once again went on finding a new job but this time, he did find a few companies where he could work but, the company owners did not want Gabriel to work there because his interview did not go well. Days passed, Gabriel had enough of this non-sense. He screamed at himself, "If I didn't find a job for me in less than two days, I would start my own business!" he continued "Well, that's a great idea. I can start my own company now that I have tons of money." He then shouted and smiled and said, "I can start my own company. Why didn't I think of this before?!"

And so, he did. He started his own company but, took a while to do this. He wanted a self-made name for his company, something that was unique. He came up with various names like Red Apple, Jefferson Electronics and Corporations which seem quite unfamiliar, probably because his imagination was different than others. He then finally came up with a proper business name 'Global Enterprises' and that's exactly what he named his company. It was an electronic company that Gabriel owned.

At the start, not that many people used to work in Gabriel's company and was short of customers as it was not much of a famous company. This is totally what Gabriel did not want to happen. His dream was to see his company full of workers and customers and wanted it to become popular as soon as possible. Now to make it popular, Gabriel told all of the people working in his company to think about it and if they managed to find a solution, they could tell it to him in his cabin. Gabriel sat there for hours in his cabin completing his work and hoping that someone in his office would come and give a solution to the problem.

Surprisingly, a manager from his company did come to Gabriel's cabin bringing a solution to the problem. "Boss!" he said "I have an idea. We can launch a product and advertise it."

"And what kind of product can we launch?" questioned Gabriel.

"Maybe an electronic device like headphones since, this is an electronic company." replied the manager.

"Do it and show it to me." said Gabriel.

It took a while to launch headphones and advertise them but after it was done, the manager showed the headphones and the advertisement to Gabriel before launching as they were told to do so. Gabriel eagerly checked the quality of the headphones and the advertisement and approved to launch them and really hoped that it would make his company famous.

Every single person who bought these headphones had a really great hearing experience. They all loved the product and gave a five-star rating to it. The next day, Gabriel got a phone call from one of the most famous companies in the world. He picked up the call and someone immediately started speaking, "Hello, am I talking to the owner of Global Enterprises?"

"Yeah!" said Gabriel "This is Gabriel Jefferson, the owner of Global Enterprises."

The person then told Gabriel that he wanted to buy hundered headphones. Gabriel exclaimed with joy that his deliverymen can surely deliver it to him. And after delivering those headphones, Gabriel's business started to grow. He started selling and advertising more and more products which made his company famous. It felt like something Gabriel could only imagine. Earlier, he dreamt about his company getting famous and later, it actually happened. A tear of joy appeared in his face.

Many other famous companies bought products from Global Enterprises because of the stunning looks and quality of those products. The number of workers in his company increased the more it became famous and earned thousands of dollars from a company he could call his own.

9

The Family of Gabriel

Gabriel was talking to one of employees of his company. He said to the employee that he was pretty tired of working for that long in the office and he also had to do tons of work the next day. The employee reminded Gabriel that the next day was a holiday so, he didn't have to do work. "Oh yeah! I forgot about that." said Gabriel "See you next week!"

They both left the office arriving home. Gabriel smiled as he thought about going out the next day back to his hometown as he promised himself way back that he wouldn't go back to his hometown, New York, until and unless he makes a big change. And guess what, he did make a big change and also completed an accomplishment he could only dream of by becoming a company owner and buying a house. But he wasn't too excited for it as he still had to visit alone as he still had no family nor friends.

He sat on the aero plane, on his way to New York. He looked through the window of the plane and was really excited to see New York after ten years. When the aero plane landed to New York, Gabriel took his first step on the ground, and then the second step and proudly looked around. "Beautiful!" whispered Gabriel under his breath.

So, he went inside his hotel kept his luggage and started roaming around in a street, not exactly knowing where he wanted to go. He kept on walking for a long time until he saw an old lady trying to cross the road and decided to help her in doing so. After crossing the road with the old lady, she looked at Gabriel to say, 'Thank you.' but the moment she looked at him, she saw the scar on his forehead and remembered something. She looked at the scar closely and knew that she knows Gabriel. "What's your name?" curiously asked the old lady.

"I'm Gabriel Jefferson." replied Gabriel.

"And you're 28, right?" asked the old lady.

Gabriel was confused and wondered how she knew his age if she doesn't even know his name. "How do you know my age?" questioned Gabriel.

"Because I know you were born 28 years ago on the seventeenth of February." said the old lady "You might have been adopted, right?"

"Yes, if you didn't know my name then how do you know all that about me?" asked Gabriel "Who are you?"

"Me knowing your age is not that important. I don't know your name but, I do know you since the day you were born. I'm your mother." said the old lady, clarifying the answer to Gabriel's question.

Gabriel was totally amazed after hearing that and at first, did not believe whatever the old lady had just spoken. He didn't believe that the old lady was his mother and asked, "How can you say you're my mother? Do you have any proof?"

"Well, if I wasn't your mother, how did I know your age and your birthday?" said the old lady "Why aren't you believing me? Your dad looks just like you."

"Then show me my dad's place. Where is he?" asked Gabriel.

"He's at home. I can take you there." said the old lady. The old lady then took Gabriel to where she lived and after arriving, the old lady rang the doorbell and an old man opened the door who was Gabriel's father. He looked at Gabriel and asked who he was. "Look at the scar on his forehead." said the old lady. He looked at the scar and was surprised. The old man actually looked like Gabriel so Gabriel had no doubt left. Gabriel cried and for the first time, he called the old lady as his mom and the old man as his dad and they were contented to hear this form Gabriel's mouth. Suddenly, a question popped up in Gabriel's mind. "What exactly happened that day and why?" he asked "Why did you guys leave me?"

They looked at each other's face. "It was raining a lot that day." the old man said "Me and your mother left you near a temple. And why we left you there was because people were dying from an unknown illness in our city. Everyone was dying and we didn't want the same to happen with you so, we left you near a temple, far away. Later, someone must have come and adopted you."

"Me being with you guys has only happened because of one person." said Gabriel "BELLADONNA!"

After living in New York for a couple of days, Gabriel convinced his parents to live in Hammonton, New Jersey as that's the place where he worked. They arrived at Hammonton and that's when Gabriel decided to go to Belladonna's house to meet her one last time in order to say something. He went near the Wharton State Forest, where she lived, and after reaching to her house, he saw those two watchmen standing outside her gate with their arms locked. Gabriel asked them whether he could go inside to meet Belladonna but, the watchman told him that she wasn't home.

He waited there for hours for Belladonna to arrive. Till then he kept on walking around in slow motion. She finally arrived while sitting in an expensive car and then the moment she got out, Gabriel ran towards her and said her name. Belladonna raised her eyebrows when she saw Gabriel once again after such a long time as she was shocked. "I'm sorry." he said "I was wrong." Belladonna was totally confused about why he was sorry and also why he arrived there. "I remember what you said to me that day." he continued "You told me that my future would be full of joy and unexpected things would keep on happening with me. I'm really sorry I didn't believe you that day. Because all that you said to me back then really happened. First of all, I found a job but then eventually, I got fired. Second of all, I won a lottery and then started my own business. And then the best thing that happened to me just a few days ago is that I met my real parents. So, it proves that my future is full of joy and unexpected things."

Belladonna laughed so hard after hearing all of that. "Okay." she said "Let me tell you the truth that I never told anyone. You might know that witches like me don't exist. Just like that, people call me a witch because I change their lives by giving a potion to them and even predict their future. But actually, I'm not a witch. I'm an ordinary person who does all this. All I put in the potions is water and then I give it to them saying that this potion will change their lives but, it's not true. That's the same thing I did to you. I just say it make people see their own inner-confidence. When you came to meet me the second time, I said that your future would be full of joy and unexpected things to make you see your own-self and your inner confidence and also to make you believe that all this will actually happen to make you feel positive. But I didn't know that it actually happened to you."

Gabriel looked down toward the ground and nodded. He went back to his parents after knowing the truth of Belladonna. He welcomed his parents inside his house. His parents went inside exploring the house and that was when his mother saw the photograph of Gabriel winning the lottery and that's when she liked his house.

Gabriel and his parents decided to know each other better by asking questions and had a quality time. They kept on talking for hours and hours that day. Every morning, Gabriel wakes up, eats the food made by his mother and goes to work. After a few decades, Gabriel used to tell his grandchildren about the life he lived several years ago. He told them that he was once adopted, treated as a servant, found a job, lost the job, won a lottery, started a business and all that. He had no family and friends years ago but now, he had both. He really suffered years ago but now, he lives a happy life with his family and a group of friends.